7/19

The Fate of
the Irish Treasure:
Ireland

THE SECRET AGENTS
JACK AND MAX STALWART SERIES

THE SECRET AGENT
JACK STALWART SERIES

For more information visit
www.elizabethsingerhunt.com

The Fate of
the Irish Treasure:
Ireland

Elizabeth Singer Hunt
Illustrated by Brian Williamson

RP|KIDS
ELPHIA

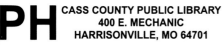

Copyright © 2019 by Elizabeth Singer Hunt

Illustrations copyright © 2019 by Brian Williamson

Running Press Kids
Hachette Book Group
1290 Avenue of the Americas, New York, NY 10104
www.runningpress.com/rpkids
@RP_Kids

Printed in the United States of America

First Edition: March 2019

Published by Running Press Kids, an imprint of Perseus Books, LLC, a subsidiary of Hachette Book Group, Inc. The Running Press Kids name and logo is a trademark of the Hachette Book Group.

The Hachette Speakers Bureau provides a wide range of authors for speaking events. To find out more, go to www. hachettespeakersbureau.com or call (866) 376-6591.

The publisher is not responsible for websites (or their content) that are not owned by the publisher.

Print book cover and interior design by Jason Kayser and Rachel Peckman.

Library of Congress Control Number: 2017963212

ISBNs: 978-1-6028-6578-5 (paperback),
978-1-6028-6577-8 (ebook)

LSC-C

10 9 8 7 6 5 4 3 2 1

For Andy, my stalwart companion.

THE WORLD

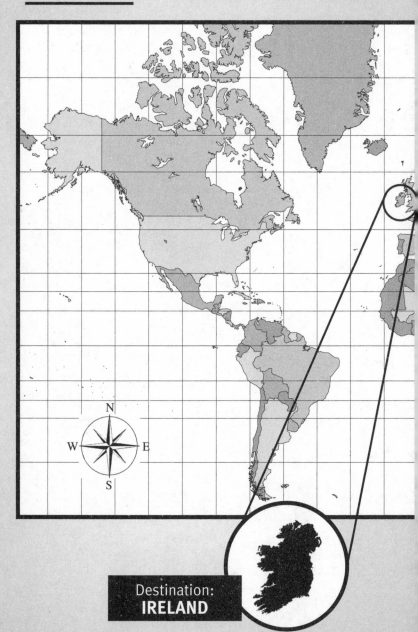

Destination:
IRELAND

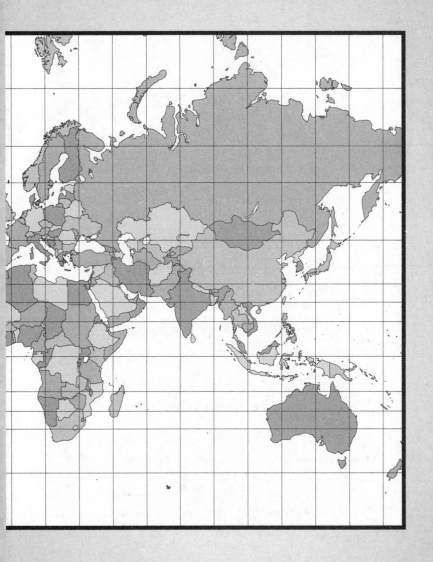

GLOBAL PROTECTION FORCE ALERT

THE WORLD'S MOST PRECIOUS TREASURES ARE UNDER ATTACK!

Secret Agents Courage and Wisdom recently thwarted an attempt to steal the *Emerald Buddha* from the Grand Palace in Thailand. The GPF believes that the mastermind behind this crime was also behind the thefts of Picasso's *Acrobat* painting and a Fabergé egg from Russia. If this is true, we have a madman on our hands.

GLOBAL PROTECTION FORCE ALERT

All agents must be prepared to travel at a moment's notice. Anyone witnessing someone or something suspicious should report it immediately to Gerald Barter, the Director of the GPF.

Louise Persnall

Louise Persnall
Assistant to Gerald Barter

THINGS YOU'LL FIND IN EVERY BOOK

Global Protection Force (GPF): The GPF is a worldwide force of junior secret agents whose aim is to protect the world's people, places, and possessions. It was started in 1947 by a man named Ronald Barter, who wanted to stop criminals from harming things that mattered in the world. When Ronald died, under mysterious circumstances, his son Gerald took over. The GPF's main offices are located somewhere in the Arctic Circle.

Watch Phone: The GPF's Watch Phone is worn by GPF agents around their wrists. It can make and receive phone calls, send and receive messages, play videos, unlock the Secret Agent Book Bag, and track an agent's whereabouts. The Watch Phone also carries the GPF's Melting Ink Pen. Just push the button to the left of the screen to eject this lifesaving gadget.

Secret Agent Book Bag: The GPF's Secret Agent Book Bag is licensed only to GPF agents. Inside are hi-tech gadgets necessary to foil bad guys and escape certain death. To unlock and lock, all an agent has to do is place his or her thumb on the zipper. The automatic thumbprint reader will identify him or her as the owner.

GPF Tablet: The GPF Tablet is a tablet computer used by GPF agents at home. On it, agents can access the GPF secure website, send encrypted e-mails, use the agent directory, and download mission-critical data.

Whizzy: Whizzy is Jack's magical miniature globe. Almost every night at 7:30 p.m., the GPF uses him to send Jack the location of his next mission. Jack's parents don't know that Whizzy is anything but an ordinary globe. Jack's brother, Max, has a similar buddy on his bedside table named "Zoom."

The Magic Map: The Magic Map is a world map that hangs on every GPF agent's wall. Recently, it was upgraded from wood to a hi-tech, unbreakable glass. Once an agent places the country shape in the right spot, the map lights up and transports him or her to his or her mission. The agent returns precisely one minute after he or she left.

DESTINATION: IRELAND

Ireland is called the "Emerald Isle" because of its lush green countryside. Green is the symbolic color of the country.

More than 6 million people live in Ireland. Dublin is Ireland's capital city.

Politically, Ireland is divided into two parts. Northern Ireland is a part of the United Kingdom. The Republic of Ireland is an independent state.

St. Patrick brought Christianity to Ireland more than 1,500 years ago. He is celebrated every year on St. Patrick's Day, which is on March 17.

The "shamrock" is a popular Irish symbol. This three-leaf clover represents the Father, Son, and Holy Spirit of the Christian religion.

The Irish wolfhound is the official dog of Ireland. It's also the tallest dog breed. It can grow to be thirty-four inches (86 cm) at the neck. It originally hunted wolves.

Potatoes are a common ingredient in Irish dishes. They were brought to the island in the 1500s.

Ireland has no snakes. They weren't quick enough to make it to the island before the seas separated Ireland from its neighboring countries.

The *Guinness World Records* started in Ireland. It was named after a director of the Guinness Brewery company, who wanted to make a book of achievements. It was first published in 1955.

The *Book of Kells* is one of Ireland's greatest national treasures.

★

It's an illustrated manuscript of the life and teachings of Jesus Christ.

★

The book was created by monks more than 1,100 years ago.

★

The pages are made from calf skin. Colors like red, yellow, blue, green, and gold are used throughout.

Animals and mythical creatures also appear.

★

For hundreds of years, the *Book of Kells* was kept at the Abbey of Kells in northeast Ireland.

★

Today, the book is on display at Trinity College Library in Dublin.

★

Trinity College is Ireland's oldest university. It was founded in 1592.

GIANT'S CAUSEWAY: FACTS AND FIGURES

The "Giant's Causeway" is a geologic rock formation in Northern Ireland.

★

It contains about 40,000 hexagonal "steps" of differing heights.

★

The causeway extends into the sea toward Scotland.

★

Legend has it that an Irish giant named Fionn mac Cumhaill built the steps, so that he could battle the Scottish giant, Benandonner. But Benandonner changed his mind and fled. He destroyed the steps closest to Scotland so that mac Cumhaill couldn't follow him.

The causeway is actually the result of volcanic eruptions. The rock is basalt.

★

The Giant's Causeway is a UNESCO World Heritage Site. That means it's been identified as a special place that needs to be celebrated and preserved.

THE STALWART FAMILY

Jack Stalwart: Nine-year-old Jack Stalwart works as a secret agent for the Global Protection Force, or GPF. Jack originally joined the GPF to find and rescue his brother, Max, who'd disappeared on one of his missions. Eventually, Jack tracked Max to Egypt, where he saved him *and* King Tut's diadem, or crown.

Max Stalwart: Twelve-year-old Max is a GPF agent too. He was recruited after filling out a questionnaire online, and pledging his young life to protect "that which cannot protect itself." Max's specialty within the GPF is cryptography, which is the ability to write and crack coded messages. Recently, Max narrowly escaped death in Egypt, while protecting King Tut's diadem.

John Stalwart: John Stalwart is the patriarch of the family. He's an aerospace engineer, who recently headed up the Mars Mission Program. For many months, the GPF had fooled John and his wife, Corinne, into thinking that their oldest son, Max, was at a boarding school in Switzerland. Really, Max was on a top secret mission in Egypt. When that mission ended, Max's "boarding school" closed, and he returned home for good. John is an American and his wife, Corinne, is British, which makes Jack and Max a bit of both.

Corinne Stalwart: Corinne Stalwart is the family matriarch. She's kind, loving, and fair. She's also totally unaware (as is her husband) that her two sons are agents for the Global Protection Force. In her spare time, Corinne volunteers at the boys' school, and studies Asian art.

GPF GADGET INSTRUCTION MANUAL

Noggin Mold: This flexible piece of plastic molds to an agent's head to form a usable helmet. Perfect when using the Flyboard, Scatta-Scooter, Torpedo, or any other GPF moving vehicle.

Heli-Drone Prototype: The GPF's Heli-Drone Prototype is a small two-person helicopter currently undergoing testing. It contains the latest hi-tech surveillance equipment including LIDAR, which can uncover hidden structures in the forest. Unlike other drone crafts, the Heli-Drone is flown by agents from the inside. Its power comes from a lithium-ion battery that needs to be charged. In case of emergency, there are two ejector buttons, one for each seat.

Map Mate app: When you're lost or need to get somewhere fast, use the GPF's Map Mate app. This clever app receives signals from satellites in space to give you a map of any country, city, or town in the world. It can also show you how to get from one place to the other using directional arrows to guide the way.

The Flyboard: When you need help getting somewhere faster than your feet will take you, use the GPF's Flyboard. The Flyboard looks like a skateboard, but has two hydrogen-powered jets at the back. Just snap it together and hop on. Push the word "air" on your Watch Phone to fly, "blades" to skate on ice, or "wheels" to speed on the ground.

Chapter 1
Miss Murphy

SWOOSH!

The door to the tour bus opened. Jack Stalwart stepped out and onto the ground. Behind him were his older brother, Max, and four other students. They and their teacher chaperones had just arrived for a three-day field trip to Dublin, Ireland.

"Gather up," said Miss Murphy.

Miss Catriona Murphy was Jack and

1

Max's art history teacher. She was twenty-five years old with short black hair and bright green eyes. Although she was new to the boys' school, she'd already become everyone's favorite teacher.

Beyond being interesting, Miss Murphy was *cool*. In her spare time, she did rock climbing and competed in endurance races. In fact, Miss Murphy had just

finished one of the toughest triathlons in
the world. Her academic interest was
Irish art, which is why they were in
Dublin in the first place. She wanted to
share the sights and sounds of the city
with her students.

Miss Murphy did a quick head count.
There was Jack and Max, Daniel Smith,
Julie Egham, Edward Brown, and Beth

Williams. All of the kids were between 9 and 12 years old.

"Let's take a group photo," said Miss Murphy, motioning for everyone to get together.

Jack and Max stood at the back and hammed it up for the camera. After the photo, Miss Murphy thumbed to the large, gray rectangular building over her shoulder. A sign out front read:

TRINITY COLLEGE LIBRARY DUBLIN
VISIT THE BOOK OF KELLS

"That's where the *Book of Kells* is kept," she said with a wink.

Jack knew all about the famous *Book of Kells*. Miss Murphy had been talking about it for weeks. The book contained "illuminated" drawings about the life and teachings of Jesus Christ.

It was "illuminated" because many of the drawings were painted in real gold. Since Jack was a bit of an artist himself,

he could appreciate how special it was. The *Book of Kells* was created by monks in the ninth century, which meant it was more than 1,100 years old. It was known as "Ireland's greatest cultural treasure."

"We've already had a long day of traveling," said Miss Murphy. "What do you say we check into the hotel?"

Miss Murphy pointed to the green-painted hotel across the road. It was called the "Lucky Leprechaun." Next to its name was an image of a friendly leprechaun, or sprite.

In addition to Miss Murphy, there was another chaperone on the trip—Ms. Humphries.

Ms. Humphries was a grumpy old woman who wore a big gold ring on one of her fingers. Whenever a student misbehaved, she would whack her ring on the top of their head. Jack had never felt it, but other students were frequent recipients. Daniel Smith, in particular, was familiar with the "sting of the ring."

THWACK!

"Yow!" squealed Daniel.

Jack turned around to see Daniel rubbing the top of his head.

"Look both ways before you cross the street!" barked Ms. Humphries.

"Yes, Ms. Humphries," said Daniel as he safely scurried across the road. While Miss Murphy was everyone's favorite teacher, Ms. Humphries was the least.

After checking into their rooms, everyone met downstairs for dinner in the hotel café. Jack ordered "colcannon," a dish made with mashed potatoes and cabbage. Max tried the "Irish stew." For dessert, the students shared a bite of "moss pudding," a fluffy sweet made from red seaweed.

"Yummy," said Jack as he dug in. Jack and Max's favorite part of any meal was dessert.

After dinner, Miss Murphy and Ms. Humphries escorted the students to their rooms.

"Let's meet in the lobby first thing tomorrow," said Miss Murphy.

"Eight a.m. sharp!" said Ms. Humphries.

After saying "good night," Jack and Max made their way to their room. They stayed up late talking about the latest soccer scores and by 10 p.m., they were fast asleep.

Chapter 2
The Unfortunate News

At 7:30 a.m., Jack and Max's alarm went off. They brushed their teeth, got dressed, and made their way to the lobby as instructed. As soon as they got there, they could tell that something was wrong. Ms. Humphries looked annoyed, and the other students were confused.

PING!

It was Ms. Humphries's phone. She looked down at the text on her screen.

"Running late?" she scowled.

Jack figured the text was from Miss Murphy.

Through the hotel window, Jack spied at least twenty Irish police cars in front of Trinity College Library.

Jack turned to Daniel.

"What's going on?" he asked.

Daniel shrugged his shoulders.

One of the lobby staff turned on the TV. There was a female reporter holding a microphone on the screen. She was standing in front of the library with the words BREAKING NEWS beneath her.

"Ireland's greatest cultural treasure—the Book of Kells—*was stolen last night," she announced. "Authorities are on the scene trying to piece together the clues."*

Jack and the others gasped. Ms.

Humphries rolled her eyes. "How inconvenient." she mumbled.

For Jack the news was more than "inconvenient." The theft of the *Book of Kells* was a serious crime. Just as Jack was wondering if he and Max might be assigned to the case, his Watch Phone pinged. As soon as he saw the text, he knew the answer.

Chapter 3
Mr. Pink

Jack and his brother, Max, were secret agents for the Global Protection Force, or GPF. Almost nightly, they were sent on missions around the globe to battle evil villains and protect the world's most priceless treasures.

Normally, the boys would receive their assignments while at home. Each of them had a miniature globe in their room that gave them the location of their next mission. They also had a Magic Map that transported them there.

But on rare occasions, the GPF needed to send an agent somewhere close to where they already were. In these cases, the GPF sent a "handler." The handler's job was to take the agent from their current situation and deliver them to their mission location.

The text Jack had received said:

Mr. Pink is on his way.

Mr. Pink was Jack and Max's handler. Jack and Max had met Mr. Pink before at a top secret GPF orientation. The thing that Jack remembered most about the man was that he didn't like being touched.

As Jack looked out the window, he saw

a strange-looking person walking toward the hotel.

The man was wearing a finely tailored black suit and shiny brown shoes. His hair was slicked back with gel, and his face was chiseled and serious. Covering his eyes were dark sunglasses. But these weren't ordinary sunglasses. These were the GPF's "Camera Shades."

The GPF's Camera Shades could take photos or videos of unsuspecting people. The files could be downloaded to an agent's Watch Phone. Or, sent directly to the GPF. Jack had no doubt that the man wearing the Camera Shades was Mr. Pink.

Mr. Pink entered the hotel and made his way to Ms. Humphries. She was scolding poor Daniel again, so her back was turned. Mr. Pink announced his presence by clearing his throat. Ms.

Humphries didn't appreciate the
interruption.

"Can I help you?" she hissed, turning
around.

"I'm here to collect my children," he
said in a wooden voice.

Jack and Max wanted to laugh. There
was nothing cuddly about Mr. Pink.

Ms. Humphries's eyebrows furrowed.
Her lips pursed.

"And *who* are your children?" she
asked.

Jack decided to help him out.

"Hi, Dad," said Jack, giving Mr. Pink a friendly smack on the back. Mr. Pink winced.

"Whoops," thought Jack to himself. He'd forgotten about Mr. Pink's little issue.

"Hello, . . . son," said Mr. Pink through gritted teeth. He smacked Jack on the back, shoving him a few feet forward.

Ms. Humphries's eyes narrowed. She looked from Mr. Pink to the boys and back again. The man looked nothing like his "sons." He didn't even look like a typical dad.

"Our dad works for the government," said Max. "That's why he's a bit serious."

"I see," said Ms. Humphries. "This is all so *sudden*."

"I'm sorry for that," said Mr. Pink. "Their mother has taken ill."

Jack and Max knew this wasn't true, but they decided to play along.

"Is it serious?" said Jack, wringing his hands.

"Is she going to be all right?" said Max, pretending to tear up.

Both boys had done at bit of acting at school. In fact, they were pretty good at

it. Seeing Jack's and Max's reactions, Ms. Humphries's became much more sympathetic.

"Is there anything I can do?" she asked.

"I'll need to take the boys," said Mr. Pink. "I'll send someone by later to collect their things."

Ms. Humphries quickly grabbed a clipboard from her bag.

"You'll need to sign this," she said. It was a parent's sign-out sheet.

"Certainly," said Mr. Pink. He pulled a pen from the inside of his jacket and put an "X" on the dotted line. He handed the clipboard back to Ms. Humphries.

She stared at the odd signature for a few moments.

"I guess—uh—this will be fine," she said.

Ms. Humphries bent over to put the clipboard away. By the time she looked up again, the boys and Mr. Pink were gone.

Chapter 4
The Investigation

Jack, Max, and Mr. Pink crossed the road
and headed to the Trinity College Library.
The female reporter that Jack had seen
on the TV was still out front reporting
the news. Blue and white "crime scene"
tape had been placed around the
building. Mr. Pink quickly unlocked a
nearby car and pulled out a couple of
Watch Phones and Book Bags from the
back seat. He gave them to Jack and

Max, who strapped them onto their bodies. Mr. Pink pushed a couple of onlookers aside as he led the boys underneath the tape and through the front door.

As soon as they entered, a short bald man with large front teeth rushed over to greet them.

He extended his hand to Jack and Max and shook theirs so enthusiastically that he rattled both of their bodies.

"Thanks for coming," he said.

Mr. Pink slinked out of the library and left.

"I'm Killian Doyle, the director of the library," said the man. "I'm so glad that you're here," he added, nearly out of breath. "The police and I are absolutely baffled."

Mr. Doyle hurriedly motioned for Jack and Max to follow him. He led the boys from the entrance and into the library's "Long Room." This was the main room of the library. As soon as they saw it, the brothers' mouths gaped open. It was absolutely beautiful.

The Long Room was more than 200 feet long. Hundreds of thousands of books were stacked on wooden shelves

two stories high. Busts of famous thinkers flanked the main walkway, and dark wood paneling covered the arched ceiling above. In the middle were a series of glass cases that showcased some of the most famous literary works in the world.

Mr. Doyle led the brothers to one in particular. Two police officers—one man and one woman— were standing over the case. There was nothing inside. The man was dusting for fingerprints. The woman was looking over his shoulder.

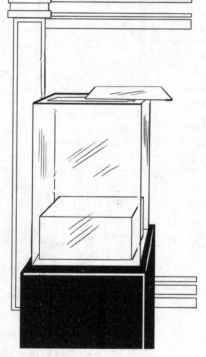

"This is where the *Book of Kells* was kept," said Mr. Doyle.

The top of the case had been sliced off. Jack and Max surveyed the cut. The lines weren't jagged. Instead, they were smooth.

"Looks like the thief used some kind of a laser," said Max.

Mr. Doyle nodded in agreement.

"That's what the police think," he said.

As they were talking, the male officer turned to the female one.

"Nothing here, boss," he said.

"Let's take it back to the lab anyway," said the woman.

The two officers left. Mr. Doyle let out a big sigh.

"That probably means the crook wore gloves," he said, lifting his eyes in exasperation.

"Tell us about your security," said Max. In addition to codebreaking, Max had an interest in hi-tech security systems.

"Every night before I leave," said Mr. Doyle, "I do a sweep of the library to make sure there aren't any stragglers."

Mr. Doyle carried on.

"Then I turn the motion sensors on," he said. "They cover every inch of the floor. If anyone were to set foot in the library at night, the alarms would go off

and the police would be immediately notified."

"Did any of them go off last night?" asked Max.

"Not a one," said Mr. Doyle.

Max noticed the 360-degree security cameras mounted to the second-floor railings. They rotated like eyeballs to film

everything from the floors to the windows to the ceiling. Max pointed to them.

"What about those?" asked Max.

"They didn't see anything," said Mr. Doyle. "But from five thirty to five forty-five a.m. the filming was interrupted."

Jack and Max looked at each other.

"That must have been when the crook stole the *Book of Kells*," said Jack.

According to Jack's Watch Phone, it was 8:45 a.m.—three hours since the theft.

Max looked to the windows on either side of the Long Room.

"Are your windows armed?" asked Max.

Mr. Doyle nodded.

"But nothing was tripped last night," he said.

Jack scratched his head. He was stumped. He couldn't figure out how the thief had stolen the *Book* without opening the windows or doors and walking on the

floor. That was, until he spied a small skylight high up on the ceiling.

Mr. Doyle caught Jack staring at it.

"I doubt the crook came in that way. It's one hundred feet off the ground!"

"You'd be surprised," said Max, who was now studying the skylight, too. He turned to Mr. Doyle.

"Have you ever seen *Mission Impossible*?" he asked.

Mr. Doyle stared at him blankly.

In the movie, the main character steals a top-secret document from a vault by lowering himself down by a rope and never touching the floor.

Jack and Max had an idea how the thief got the *Book of Kells*. Now, they just needed to prove it.

"How do we get onto the roof?" asked Jack.

"This way," said Mr. Doyle, leading the boys towards a nearby hallway.

He unlocked a chunky wooden door with one of the thirty keys dangling from a chain on his trousers. Once through, the trio climbed a twisting set of stairs to a metal door. Mr. Doyle opened it and they stepped on the roof.

Jack and Max zeroed in on the skylight and knelt down next to it.

"It's bigger in person," said Jack.

"Definitely large enough for a man to fit through," said Max.

Mr. Doyle leaned over the boys'

shoulders and watched them do their work.

Jack and Max slipped on their GPF Investigation Gloves. These thin white gloves allowed agents to touch things without leaving their prints.

Jack pried open the hatch.

"Look," said Jack, pointing to some

deep grooves and scratches on the edge of the frame. "It looks like the thief attached some sort of winch."

"That would explain the marks," said Max.

"It would also explain how he managed to lower himself down and up," said Jack.

"Using a rope," added Mr. Doyle. "Just like in the movie."

"And I bet he used a scrambling device," said Jack, "to interrupt the security camera signal."

"The question is," said Max, "which way did he go after he took the treasure?"

Jack and Max gazed across the roof.

There, in the dust was a set of footprints. One was coming toward the skylight. The other was heading away.

Jack and Max followed the prints until

they stopped at the walled edge of the
roof. They looked over it. On the other
side was a fire escape ladder that led to
an alleyway below.

Jack radioed the GPF and asked them
to pull camera footage from the alley.
Then he told them to come and analyze
the footprints on the roof.

Although the Irish police had a team of
their own, the GPF had a device that
could scan and analyze footprints. They
could compare the marking from the roof

with the thousands of prints in its database and identify the shoe's size, as well as its brand, in minutes.

Jack turned to Mr. Doyle.

"A team of GPF investigators will be arriving soon," said Jack. "Can you be here to greet them?"

"Sure," said Mr. Doyle. "But where will you two be?"

Jack and Max smiled.

"Catching the crook," they said together, as they stepped over the wall and disappeared to the other side.

Chapter 5
The Escape

After scrambling down the ladder, Jack and Max found themselves in a dead end alley. Behind them was the ladder. In front of them was a cobblestone lane of shops, pubs, and restaurants.

"The crook could have easily blended into the streets of Dublin from here," said Max.

The boys looked around for clues. On the ground near Jack's foot was a single

tire track heading out of the alley and
into the lane. Jack bent down to get a
better look.

"It's fatter than a bicycle tire," said
Jack. "This looks like a motorbike tread."

Besides the tread, Jack noticed
something else. There was a CCTV

camera mounted on the brick building opposite the fire escape.

This time, Jack contacted the GPF's surveillance team. He asked them to tap into the camera footage from the alley around 5:45 a.m. and try to isolate the crook.

It took the surveillance team ten minutes, but when they called back, they had helpful news. A masked figure dressed in black was seen leaving the alley on a black motorbike at 5:50 a.m. From there, he drove north. The GPF knew this because other cameras in the city had been able to track his movements too. The last time the masked thief was seen was at 7:30 a.m. near the Ha'Penny Bridge.

Chapter 6
The Bridge

"Do you think he's still there?" asked Jack.

"There's only one way to find out," said Max, tapping the Map Mate app on his Watch Phone.

Max input the name "Ha'Penny Bridge" and waited as the app drew a map of Dublin with directions. A green dot marked their start point. A red dot marked the end.

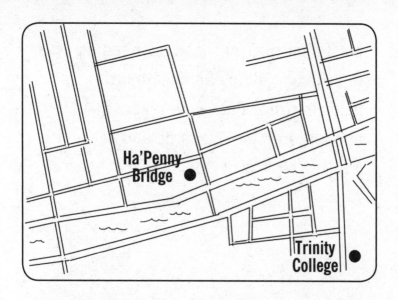

"It'll take twenty minutes to walk," said Max.

"We don't have the time," said Jack.

There was only one way the boys could get there quickly, and that was with the GPF's Flyboard. The Flyboard was a skateboard with two hydrogen-powered jets at the back. Since there were cobblestone streets in their way, the brothers activated the "air" feature. Their Flyboards rose a foot off the ground.

Jack and Max put a floppy piece of

plastic on their heads and waited as their GPF Noggin Molds hardened into helmets. Once they were ready, they hopped on their Flyboards and set off into the streets of Dublin.

Chapter 7
The Surprise Attack

Using their bodies to navigate, Jack and Max veered right from the lane and headed north. After Westmoreland Street, they hung a left. In less than five minutes, they were facing Ha'Penny Bridge.

Ha'Penny Bridge was a white-painted bridge that crossed the River Liffey, one of Ireland's biggest rivers. Every day, tens of thousands of people used the

Ha'Penny Bridge to get from one side of the river to the other.

Jack and Max hovered on the western side. They surveyed the top of the bridge and the structure underneath. As far as they could tell, there was no sign of the crook anywhere.

It was then that Max spotted a black motorbike parked on the opposite side

of the river. Directly below the bike was a series of steps leading to a blue-and-white boat docked in the water. The GPF surveillance team had seen a motorbike leaving the scene.

"Do you think that's his hideout?" asked Jack.

Max pulled out his Google Goggles.

"Let's find out," he said. The GPF's Google Goggles were hi-tech binoculars that could see far distances and through walls. Max scanned the outside of the boat.

"There's no sign of the thief on deck," he said.

Max changed the setting to "X-Ray." His vision zoomed to the inside of the boat. As soon as it did, he saw the crook. Just like in the surveillance video, he was dressed in black and wearing a black mask.

Normally in a situation like this, the boys would call for reinforcements. But there was no time. The thief was strapping a backpack to his back and standing up from a chair.

"He's getting ready to leave!" said Max.

The boys flew into action. They quickly

sailed over the bridge, put away their Flyboards, and pulled out their GPF Tornadoes. The GPF Tornado was a gadget capable of catching up to three villains at a time. All they had to do was push a button and a rope would come out, wrapping the thief up like a sausage. With a Tornado in each of their hands, there was no way the crook could get away. Rather than wait for the thief to come out, the brothers decided to burst inside. That way, the element of surprise would be on their side.

But as soon as they opened the door to the cabin, they were sprayed with a toxic substance that blinded them and made their eyes feel like they were on fire.

"Yoooowwwwww!" said Jack as he squealed in pain.

"Noooo!" hollered Max as he tried to rub the sting out.

While Jack and Max fumbled around, the thief snatched the boys' Tornadoes and ripped their Book Bags off their backs. Their Watch Phones were cut from their wrists and they were dragged to the upper deck. The next thing they knew, Jack and Max were shoved from behind and into the river below.

SPLASH!

Chapter 8
The Paddy Boat

Jack's head broke above water. He was gasping for air.

"Max?!" he cried out.

There was no answer.

"Are you okay?" yelled Jack.

He couldn't see anything, but he could hear the sound of splashing nearby.

"I'm all right!" hollered Max. "Are you okay?"

"Yeah," responded Jack.

Thankfully, the water from the river was lapping at their eyes, slowly helping their vision come back.

"We have to get back to the boat!" cried Jack. Not only did they have to catch the thief, they had to get their top secret Book Bags and gadgets.

The brothers started to swim for the boat. But almost as soon as they did, the

boat peeled away from the dock. It sped off in the opposite direction. Jack tried to swim faster. But it was no use. The only way to catch up to the thief was to get a boat of their own. Unfortunately, there were no available boats in sight.

Just then, they heard a loud rumbling sound coming from behind. It was a powerboat. Thinking fast, the boys waved furiously, trying to flag it down. The driver saw them and pulled up alongside Jack and Max. He was a middle-aged man with a cheery face and dark brown hair.

"You lads out for a swim?" he said
jokingly. The man spoke with a heavy
Irish accent.

Jack and Max chuckled nervously. They
thought about telling him the truth. But

they figured he wouldn't believe that they were a couple of secret agent kids. So, Jack came up with a believable fib.

"My brother and I accidentally fell overboard," said Jack. He pointed to the boat disappearing around the bend. "Our parents have no idea."

"Goodness me!" said the man.

He reached down to Jack and Max and yanked them out of the river and onto the boat. It was then that they got a good look at the man's trousers. They were the colors of the Irish flag—bright orange, green, and white plaid. Jack's eyes opened wide.

"Paddy Finnegan's the name," he said, brushing the dirty river water from his pants. "Let's get you back to your parents."

Paddy put the boat into drive, and the three of them sped off.

Chapter 9
The Chase

Paddy's boat had a powerful engine. It took only thirty seconds for the trio to catch up to the other boat. Paddy pulled in close behind it and honked his horn. He grabbed a nearby megaphone.

"I have your boys," he said, his voice booming. "Slow down so they can board."

Surprisingly, the thief did what Paddy suggested. He pulled over to the side of

the river, next to a pedestrian walkway.
But instead of waiting for Jack and Max,
the thief killed the engine, jumped out of
the boat, and began to run.

"Huh?" said Paddy, scratching his
head. "Where's your dad off to?"

Paddy parked his boat along the walkway too, just behind the other boat.

"And why's he got a mask on?" he added.

Jack signaled to his brother. He'd go after the crook while Max retrieved their belongings from the other boat.

"It's just a little game of 'hide-and-seek' that we play," said Jack, climbing out of the boat and trying to act natural.

"Thanks for the ride," said Max, climbing out too.

"Don't mention it," said Paddy, tipping his head to the boys. "Take care."

Chapter 10
The Close Call

By now, the crook was several blocks
ahead, and sprinting fast. Jack ran along
the walkway and jumped over a railing in
his way.

BLAM!

He came down hard on the pavement.
Jack sprinted past a yellow-painted sweet
shop and a red hotel with the Irish flag
out front.

The crook hooked a left and ran across an elaborately designed bridge. Jack followed in hot pursuit, passing by sculptures of mythical creatures on tall green lanterns.

The crook headed past Parliament Street and toward Dublin's City Hall. He stopped at a car park in front of the public library.

At the same time, an elderly woman was getting into her red car. The thief grabbed the keys out of her hands, shoved her aside, and jumped into the driver's seat.

"Help!" shouted the lady as she pointed her bony finger at him. "He's stealing my car!"

The thief started up the engine and peeled out of the car park. The car swerved, narrowly missing Jack, as he burst onto the scene. Jack noticed a white sticker on the back bumper. It said:

HONK IF YOU'RE OVER 80!

Jack rushed over to the woman.

"Are you okay?" he asked.

"Yes," she said. "But I want my car back! I've had it since I was 62!"

There was the sound of footsteps behind Jack. He turned around ready to strike. It was Max. Max was panting and out of breath.

"Did you find them?" asked Jack. He was talking about their Book Bags, Tornadoes, and Watch Phones.

Max shook his head. "They weren't on the boat," he said. "He might have dumped them in the river."

The elderly woman stood listening to the boys, half frustrated and half confused.

"What the devil are you two talking about?!" she said, stamping her foot. "I need to find my car!"

"Sorry, ma'am," said Jack.

The boys quickly escorted the woman into the library, where a friendly receptionist agreed to look after her.

Chapter 11
The Buddy Call

With the old lady taken care of, the boys headed outside. Luckily for them, there was an old-fashioned pay phone. Jack picked up the receiver and dialed "O" for the "Operator." He gave the woman the GPF's emergency number. Once connected, Jack found himself speaking to Buddy. Jack had worked with Buddy when he and his brother were tracking the thieves who'd taken the *Emerald*

Buddha in Thailand.

"Hiya, Buddy," said Jack. "Long time, no speak."

Buddy laughed at the joke. "Hello, Secret Agent Courage," said Buddy. The GPF's voice recognition software had identified him as an agent with the GPF.

"Secret Agent Wisdom and I are in Ireland," explained Jack. "We're trying to get the thief who took the *Book of Kells*."

"Gotcha," said Buddy.

"Unfortunately," said Jack, "we're without our Book Bags and Watch Phones."

"That's not good," said Buddy.

"And the crook has taken off in a red Toyota," said Jack. "It has a white sticker on the back that says 'Honk if you're over eighty!' At this point, we have no way of following him."

"I'll try to see if I can find him using our surveillance videos," said Buddy. "In the meantime," he said, "I might have a way for you to catch up to him."

Jack pressed his ear to the phone.

"There's a Heli-Drone prototype only blocks away," said Buddy.

Jack's eyes widened.

"How would you boys like to take it out for a spin?" asked Buddy.

"Are you kidding me?" said Jack, who couldn't believe their luck. "We'd love to!"

"Make your way to Celtic Street," said Buddy, "about four blocks north. Enter the code G-O-L-D at the hangar. Thumbprint identification should be enough to fly the drone. If I pick up anything on the red car, I'll let you know."

"Thanks," said Jack. "For all of your help."

"Go get 'em, Courage," said Buddy. And then he signed off.

Chapter 12
The Heli-Drone

Jack and Max found their way to Celtic Street and spotted the hangar in the middle of an abandoned car park. The hangar was made of aluminum and the size of a two-car garage.

Max found a keypad with the letters "A" through "Z" and the numbers "0" through "9" on the outside. He punched in the code word "G-O-L-D" and waited. The door to the hangar clicked open.

The brothers looked over their shoulders before slipping inside.

Sitting on the floor was what looked like a mini helicopter. This was the GPF's Heli-Drone. The Heli-Drone was a two-person drone outfitted with the latest hi-tech surveillance equipment. It could map an area using LIDAR, a laser-based technology that could identify hidden structures beneath the trees and the ground. The Heli-Drone could also take photos and videos as it flew overhead.

The brothers approached the aircraft.

Max placed his thumb on the identificaton pad and the hatch popped open.

Max climbed into the driver's seat, while Jack wedged himself into the seat in the back. Max surveyed the dashboard in front of him.

In the middle was an "airspeed indicator" that measured speed in miles per hour. Since the Heli-Drone was powered by a lithium-ion battery, there was also a battery power gauge to show how much energy was left. To charge it, all you had to do was plug the Heli-Drone into a power source for at least twelve hours. Below the dashboard was a joystick for steering.

One of the most remarkable features of the Heli-Drone was its ability to go

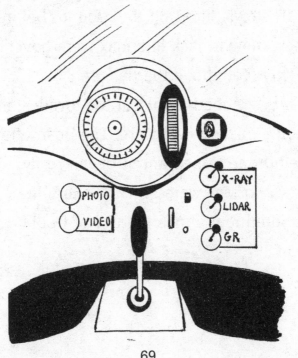

"stealth." This meant that it (and its passengers) could disappear from view. Not only was it invisible to radar, it was also invisible to the naked eye. All an agent had to do was hit the "stealth" button to activate this feature.

Max placed his thumb on the reader. As soon as it registered Max's print, the Heli-Drone's propeller began to spin. The roof hatch of the hangar opened, and the craft slowly lifted off the ground. Before they knew it, Jack and Max were hovering eighty feet above the hangar.

Max grabbed a hold of the joystick and gently pushed it forward. The nose of the Heli-Drone tipped and it began to fly. Jack and Max were now traveling one hundred feet above the city of Dublin.

Chapter 13
The Tip

"That's where he took a right," said Jack, pointing to the street leaving the library's car park.

Max maneuvered the Heli-Drone to fly along the road. Below them was Dublin Castle. They passed over City Hall and the River Liffey below.

Just then, a message lit up on the dashboard's screen.

A few seconds passed, and then Buddy appeared. It was the first time either Jack or Max had seen him in person. He was as kind and friendly-looking as his voice.

"Hello, agents," he said. "I've isolated the red car. After the public library, the thief headed north of the city and onto the M1." Jack and Max knew that the M1 was a major highway in Ireland.

"He seems to be headed toward the coast," said Buddy. "There's a 'Map Mate' in the Heli-Drone, if you need it."

"Thanks, Buddy," said Max.

"Anytime," said Buddy.

Then, Buddy signed off.

Chapter 14
The Emergency

Max activated the "Map Mate" and a map of Ireland appeared on another screen on the dash. He set their destination to the M1 and followed the directional arrows.

The boys flew for what seemed like hours. They passed over hundreds of cars, but none of them looked like the red car from Dublin. After a while, Jack saw a car that could be the one. He strained his eyes. It was the same shade of red and it had a white sticker at the back.

HONK IF YOU'RE OVER 80!

"That's it!" said Jack.

Max punched the "stealth" button. The last thing they needed was for their cover to be blown. The Heli-Drone faded from sight. Jack and Max carefully followed the thief's route as it left the M1 and drove onto smaller, less inhabited roads.

As they traveled, Max glanced at the battery's power gauge. It wasn't good news. Their energy was running low.

"We need to make a move soon," said Max.

Jack looked at the ground below. There were almost no houses. The land was barren, sometimes green and rocky.

The car continued to drive until the road came to an end. At the end of the

road was an empty car park. The thief
pulled into it and waited for a few
minutes. Then he got out and started to
run. Jack and Max looked at each other,
confused.

"Where is he going?" asked Max.

There was nothing ahead but water.
The crook was running to the northern
end of Ireland itself.

Up ahead was a flat patch of land.

"I'm going to try and land on it," said Max. "We might be able to cut him off."

But just as Max was lowering the Heli-Drone to land, flashing lights started to appear. An angry computerized voice boomed through its speakers.

ABORT!

ABORT!

ABORT!

The Heli-Drone fell thirty feet to the left, slamming Jack and Max against the side. Max threw the joystick hard to the right, trying to level things out. But it didn't work. The joystick wasn't responding.

Max looked at the Heli-Drone's battery power. It was empty. If they didn't do something fast, they were going to crash. Max looked for an emergency "eject" button. There were two, one above each of their seats. He reached back and

punched Jack's first. The hatch above
Jack opened. Jack and his seat were
catapulted from the Heli-Drone. A small
parachute opened, helping Jack float
safely to the ground.

ABORT!

ABORT!

ABORT!

The voice was still shouting at Max.
There was no time to waste. Max
punched the "eject" button above his

seat. He, too, flew out of the top, a parachute opening above his head.

Jack watched as the Heli-Drone spun several times before skidding onto the rocks below. It came to a stop with a large gash underneath. Max's chute lowered him to the ground.

Something out of the corner of Jack's eye caught his attention. It was the thief. For a moment, Jack had forgotten all about him. The boys unbuckled their seatbelts and started to run.

Chapter 15
The Giant's Causeway

The crook was racing toward a series of
tall, hexagonal, staggered rocks. Jack
recognized them immediately. This was
the Giant's Causeway. Irish legend said
that the steps had been made by a giant
named Fionn mac Cumhaill. Jack knew
that instead they had been formed from
a series of volcanic eruptions.

The thief bounded over the uneven
rocks, hopping from one to the other like

he was jumping on springs. Jack and Max
headed straight for him. But scrambling
over the rocks wasn't easy. Each one was
a different height, slowing the brothers
down.

Just then, the thief stopped in his
tracks. He turned to face the boys. He
took what looked like a small grenade
out of his vest pocket and hurled it at

Jack. The thief started running again. Jack dove to the right.

BOOM!

The device detonated, sending a small explosion of tear gas into the air. Jack started to cough immediately. The gas was making it difficult to breath. He lifted his shirt over his mouth. Then he ran through the gas and into the fresher air ahead.

Max was only fifty yards behind the thief. The thief threw another tear gas grenade over his shoulder. This one landed close to Max. It exploded, causing Max to collapse to the ground. He fell awkwardly on the rocks, twisting his ankle. Max tried to get up, but he couldn't move.

"Max!" shouted Jack, stopping in his tracks to check on his brother.

"Go ahead!" hollered Max, coughing

through the toxic air. "I'm okay!" Max
lifted his shirt over his mouth too.

Jack wasn't sure whether his brother
really was okay, but he had no choice
but to go on. Jack was their only hope
for catching the thief.

The thief began to scramble up the hill
using his hands and his feet. Jack
couldn't figure out whether he was being
lured into a trap or whether the man was
running for something on the other side
of the hill.

Within minutes, the thief was standing on top. Strangely, he no longer seemed to care about Jack. Instead, he was talking on a cell phone and staring at the sky. With the thief's attention elsewhere, Jack decided to make his move.

Jack bolted over the crest of the hill. He dove toward the thief's legs, grabbing them and toppling him to the ground. The thief was temporarily stunned. Thinking the *Book of Kells* was in his backpack, Jack reached for it. But the man kicked Jack in the elbow and then in the stomach. Jack crumpled into a ball in pain. He could barely breathe.

The thief regained his footing and stood. He left Jack on the ground and looked to the sky. Black clouds were rolling in. Jack could feel the patter of raindrops on his face. Suddenly, it began to drizzle.

Something else was making its way across the sky too. A black helicopter was heading toward the hill. Jack watched as it swooped through the rain and hovered twenty feet above them. The force of the wind from the propellers was making the grasses lay flat. It was difficult for Jack to move.

The side door to the helicopter opened and a rope ladder trickled out.

Unfortunately for Jack, this wasn't the Irish police or the GPF. This helicopter had been summoned by the crook. If Jack let the man get on board, the *Book of Kells* might be lost forever.

Jack looked down the hill to the Giant's Causeway. Max was hobbling toward the hill. But he was slow—too slow to catch up to Jack anytime soon. Jack's only hope was to delay the thief as long as he could.

But Jack had no Watch Phone, no Book Bag, and no gadgets. He didn't even have a rope that he could turn into a handcuff. There was nothing available but Jack's brains and body to stop the thief.

As the thief put his right foot on the ladder, Jack peeled himself off of the ground. He charged at the man and barreled into his side. The thief and Jack

splashed down together into a muddy
puddle.

Jack crawled on top of the thief, trying
to grab his hands. But the rain made
everything slippery. Everytime Jack tried
to grab one of his wrists, the thief
managed to pull them away.

Jack could feel his chances dwindle.
The only thing Jack could do now was
get a good look at the man. At least he
could give a description to the

authorities. Jack grabbed the man's mask and yanked it from his head.

But when Jack looked down, he got the shock of his life. The person he'd thought was a man was actually a woman. And it wasn't just any woman.

It was Miss Murphy.

Chapter 16
The Thief Revealed

Jack sat back, completely stunned. He tried to make sense of the situation.

"Surprise." She sneered.

"I—I—I don't understand," said Jack, stuttering. "Where's the thief?"

"You're looking at her," she said with a growl.

Jack couldn't compute what she was saying. Miss Murphy *couldn't* be the

person who took the *Book of Kells*. She was his art teacher after all. But then Jack remembered something. She wasn't in the lobby the morning of the theft. In fact, Ms. Humphries was annoyed because she'd received a text from Miss Murphy telling her that she'd been delayed. Had Miss Murphy sent that text to Ms. Humphries from the boat after she'd taken the *Book of Kells*?

"Are you even a teacher?" asked Jack. "Is your name Catriona Murphy?"

The woman didn't say a thing. She just smirked. Jack knew one thing. The "Miss Murphy" sitting in front of him was nothing like the one he knew. Maybe, thought Jack, she only pretended to be nice so that no one suspected her. Unfortunately, for Jack, she had another trick up her sleeve.

"Sorry, kid," she said, standing up. She
pulled a GPF's Tornado from her vest.
This was one of the gadgets she'd taken
from Jack and Max on the boat.

As soon as Jack saw it, he panicked. He
got up and started to run away.

The thief pointed it at him and pulled
the trigger. Instantly, a rope shot out,
zeroing in on Jack. It targeted his head
and shoulders first, then swirled around
his ankles. Unable to move his feet, Jack
tripped and fell to the ground with a

THUD. The only things that weren't covered by rope were Jack's eyes and mouth.

"You won't get away with this!" he shouted.

The woman looked at him and laughed.

"I already have." She sneered.

She scrambled up the rope ladder, pulled it inside the chopper, and disappeared.

Jack watched helplessly as the door to the helicopter closed. Then the woman and the *Book of Kells* vanished into the dark and stormy clouds above.

Chapter 17
The Lessons Learned

"Arrrgh!" yelled Jack in frustration.

He couldn't believe it. He and Max had been tricked. They'd also broken every rule the GPF told them to follow.

Don't trust anyone.

Follow the facts.

Never assume.

Always be on guard.

At every step of the way, the woman had outplayed them.

Max's face appeared over the edge of the hill. He made his way over to Jack. Max pulled out a pocketknife from the left heel of his boot and cut Jack free.

"You okay?" asked Max.

"Yeah," said Jack. He was lying, of course. His stomach was killing him.

Jack told his brother everything that had happened. Max was shocked.

"I can't believe it," said Max. "I never would have suspected Miss Murphy."

"She was counting on that," said Jack.

"Everyone assumed the crook was a guy."

Max shook his head. "We should have known better," he said.

The boys sat there for a moment, thinking about what to do next. They had no way of getting home or contacting the GPF. For all they knew, their Book Bags and Watch Phones were at the bottom of the River Liffey.

"Let's start walking," said Max. "Maybe we'll find someone along the way."

Chapter 18
The Return of the Boys

They trudged through the rain for an hour. Eventually, they ran into a couple out walking their dog. They borrowed the couple's cell phone and called the GPF. The GPF contacted the authorities and gave them a description of the woman. They also told them about the helicopter and the direction it was headed.

Mr. Pink was sent to collect the boys.

He drove them back to Dublin and the
Lucky Leprechaun hotel.

There, they found Ms. Humphries and
the others eating a late lunch in the
downstairs café. When Jack, Max, and
their "dad" arrived, everyone—including
Ms. Humphries—was surprised.

Mr. Pink explained that his wife had made a full and "miraculous" recovery. He asked whether his sons could rejoin the trip. Ms. Humphries gave him another form to sign. After Mr. Pink scribbled an "X," Jack and Max were welcomed back into the group. Mr. Pink left the boys with the others. By now, Jack and Max were starving.

Just then, there was a news flash on the hotel TV. The same female reporter from before appeared excitedly on the screen.

We've just received word that the police have confirmed the identity of the thief. A woman posing as a school teacher from Surrey Academy in England is suspected of stealing the Book of Kells. She brought her students on a field trip to Dublin as an excuse to carry out her elaborate plan.

This caught the attention of Ms. Humphries and the other students. Their eyes shot toward the TV.

This is a photo of the woman.

A photo flashed on the screen. It was a picture of Miss Murphy.

Ms. Humphries's fork fell out of her hand. Beth Williams's food spilled out of her mouth.

She was working under the alias of Catriona Murphy. If anyone has any information about the whereabouts of this woman, please contact the Irish police. She is still in possession of the Book of Kells. The authorities are keen to apprehend her.

Ms. Humphries looked back to the table of students. She was thinking of what to say. She composed herself and picked up her fork.

"I never liked her anyway," she said, shoveling a bit of food into her mouth. "A little too perfect, if you ask me."

Chapter 19
The News Flash

Over the next several days, Jack and Max and the others visited the famous sites of Dublin. They saw Dublin Castle and St. Patrick's Cathedral. They even visited the Leprechaun Museum.

As soon as they returned to their home in England, Jack and Max raced upstairs to Jack's room. They logged into Jack's GPF Tablet, and pulled up the GPF's secure site. They were hoping that the

woman had been caught. Unfortunately,
it wasn't good news.

GPF NEWS FLASH

*Despite the efforts of some of our best
agents, the GPF has yet to locate either
the Book of Kells or the woman who stole
it. The GPF is working closely with the CIA
and MI6 to hunt her down.*

Jack logged out. Max could tell his
brother was frustrated.

"It's not your fault," said Max, placing his hand on Jack's shoulder. "We did our best."

Jack knew that. He knew that nobody—not even a GPF agent—was perfect. But he couldn't get that woman out of his mind. Jack turned to his brother.

"If it's the last thing I do," said Jack, "I'll find her and bring her to justice. She won't get away from me again."

Chapter 20
The Mastermind's Accomplice

There was a knock at the door. The Mastermind, who had been reading the morning's paper, looked up. The door creaked open. His secretary, Linda, stuck her head inside.

"Someone to see you, sir," said Linda.

The Mastermind raised one of his white eyebrows. He nodded to tell Linda to let the person in.

The door opened wide. A female figure
brushed passed Linda. She was twenty-
five years old with short black hair. It
was Miss Murphy, although that wasn't
her real name.

"Come in," said Mastermind. His finger
beckoned her in.

She took her backpack off her back

and placed it on top of his desk. She
unzipped it, revealing the *Book of Kells*
inside. His eyes twinkled.

"Excellent work," he said, pulling a
couple of thin gloves out of his pocket.
He put them on so he wouldn't damage
the book.

He pulled the book out and opened it.

He carefully turned the pages one at a time, gazing at the illuminated drawings inside. They were glittering in gold.

"Excellent work, indeed," he said.

"It wasn't easy," said the woman. "I had a couple of agents on my tail."

The man's eyes narrowed.

"Agents?" he asked, concerned.

The woman nodded. "Jack and Max Stalwart," she said. "They were my students. I think they work for the GPF."

She pulled one of the boys' Watch Phones out of her vest.

She showed it to the man. He took it into his hand. He recognized it immediately.

"You're right," he said to her. "This *is* a GPF device."

"Obviously," she said, "I managed to get away."

"Well done," he said. "I've hired others who haven't been so lucky."

He thought back to his foiled attempt at taking the *Emerald Buddha* in Thailand. The people that he hired for that job were a bunch of buffoons.

"What did the boys look like?" asked the man.

The woman pulled a photograph out of one of her pockets. She laid it on the desk and pointed to Jack and Max at the back.

"That's them at the back," she said.

"Do you mind if I take this?" he asked, his finger pointing to the photo.

"It's all yours," she said.

The man slipped the photo in his shirt pocket.

"So what about the money?" she asked.

The man pulled an envelope out of one

of the desk drawers. He handed it to her. She checked to make sure the $300,000 was there. It was.

"Nice doing business with you," she said as she stuffed it away.

"Likewise," said the man. "I'm hoping that we can work together again soon."

"Sure thing," said the woman. "You know where to find me."

"I do," said the man.

The woman left the office.

The Mastermind carefully lifted the *Book of Kells* and placed it on a nearby shelf. It was now among some of the other treasure he'd collected—a priceless Picasso painting, a Russian Fabergé egg, and a shipwreck treasure.

The Mastermind took the photo from his pocket, and studied the two boys.

A quick call to his "mole" inside the GPF would confirm if they were indeed

agents. There were also ways to find out whether they'd been in Thailand.

Either way, the Mastermind had come to the conclusion that Jack and Max Stalwart were pests. As far as he was concerned there was only one way to deal with pests . . . and that was to exterminate them.

The Race for Gold Rush Treasure:
California (USA)

READ THE FIRST CHAPTER HERE!

Chapter 1
The Coded Letter

In a filthy Mexican jail cell, a prisoner sat
on his bed holding a letter that he'd
received that day. The note was written
in childlike handwriting. There were
twelve pink pony stickers scattered
across the page. Anyone who looked at
the note would think it was written by a
little girl. But the prisoner knew better. It
was a message from a member of his
adult gang.

He pulled the first sticker off the page. The word "MEET" was written on the page underneath. Under the second sticker was the word "AT." The third sticker revealed the time "11:30 p.m."

After removing the rest of the stickers, the man studied the message.

Meet at 11:30 p.m. tonight. Gas station 5 miles due west. Gold awaits.

The prisoner grunted with pleasure.
BANG!

The door to the cellblock clanged open against the wall behind it. A skinny prison guard sporting a handlebar mustache entered the cellblock. He walked down the hallway and checked in on each of the ten prisoners. The inmate stuffed the note into this trouser pocket before the guard arrived at his cell.

"Lights out in five minutes!" shouted the guard in Spanish.

The prisoner nodded to the man. He'd already been in the prison for sixty days. He knew the schedule. At 10 p.m. every night, the lights went out. Most of the prisoners used the time to sleep. But not this prisoner. He used the nighttime hours to prepare his escape.

As soon as he'd arrived, the man had stolen a spoon from the prison cafeteria. Every night since, he'd used it to scrape at the soft wall near the floor of his cell. Just last week, he'd managed to make a hole big enough to fit through. Now that his gang was ready for him, all the prisoner had to do was escape.

CLICK.

The lights went out.

The prisoner waited for the other

inmates to fall asleep. Then he moved
the bedside table that was covering the
hole to the side. He got down on his
hands and knees and slithered through
it. Once outside, he began to run.

In front of him was a tall barbed wire

fence. A spotlight from above was
zigzagging across the grounds. He waited
for the light to move somewhere else,
then he bolted for the fence.

He climbed it and thrust his body over the barbs. They ripped at his clothes and sliced into his skin. But the prisoner didn't care. He was Callous Carl, the toughest treasure hunter on the planet. As soon as his feet hit the ground, he ran across the Mexican desert and toward the lights of the gas station ahead.

Join Jack and Max in their other adventures...